THE WARLOCK'S STAFF

URSUS
THE CLAWED
ROAR

With special thanks to Michael Ford

To Stan and Ted

www.beastquest.co.uk

ORCHARD BOOKS
338 Euston Road, London NW1 3BH
Orchard Books Australia
Level 17/207 Kent St, Sydney, NSW 2000

A Paperback Original
First published in Great Britain in 2011

Beast Quest is a registered trademark of Beast Quest Limited
Series created by Beast Quest Limited, London

Text © Beast Quest Limited 2011
Cover and inside illustrations by Steve Sims © Orchard Books 2011

A CIP catalogue record for this book is available from
the British Library.

ISBN 978 1 40831 316 9

1 3 5 7 9 10 8 6 4 2

Printed in Great Britain by CPI Bookmarque, Croydon

Orchard Books is a division of Hachette Children's Books,
an Hachette UK company

www.hachette.co.uk

URSUS
THE CLAWED
ROAR

BY ADAM BLADE

ORCHARD

Seraph

REDWELL

THE
EASTERN
FOREST

Tom and Elenna are such fools! They thought their Quests were over and that my master was defeated. They were wrong! For now Malvel has the Warlock's Staff, hewn from the Tree of Being, and all kingdoms will soon be at his mercy.

We travel the land of Seraph, to find the Eternal Flame. And when we burn the staff in the flame, our evil magic will be unstoppable. Tom and Elenna can chase us if they wish, but they'll find more than just Beasts lying in wait. They're alone this time, with no wizard to help them.

I hope Tom and Elenna are ready to meet me again. I've been waiting a long time for my revenge.

Yours, with glee, Petra the Witch

PROLOGUE

Brendan lifted the lid off the stew pot and breathed deeply. "Smells delicious!" he said to his son Luke, who sat on the other side of the fire.

Luke pointed into the cave behind them, the entrance to the whole network where the rest of the tribe lived. "The others will pick up the scent too. They'll be hungry."

Brendan ladled stew into a bowl and handed it to Luke. "Just think," he said. "They say that people in

Avantia eat off golden platters."

Luke laughed. "Don't be silly, Father! Avantia's not even real. I've heard they sleep in feather beds too. Who would make up such a thing?"

Brendan spooned some of the broth into his mouth. "Ow! It's hot!" He sucked in cool breaths, then swallowed. "Perhaps you're right. Feathers must be itchy! A hammock's good enough for me."

Luke blew on his broth, and gazed out over the landscape of Seraph. Trees dotted the rich pastures, and cattle roamed over the plains. The sky was cloudless and hazy, and a distant lake sparkled like a sapphire.

Who needs real jewels? Luke thought.

As he watched, Ursus the Bear nosed through the bushes nearby. His glossy brown fur rippled over muscled flanks as he lumbered along. Luke and Brendan both bowed to greet the old bear who had always been their protector. No one really knew if having him around helped to guard the village, but it reassured them all to have him nearby. Ursus lifted his nose in reply. With a yawn, he disappeared back into the undergrowth. *Probably looking for a bees' nest to plunder*, thought Luke.

"In Avantia the people worship a man," said Brendan. "They call him a 'king'."

"These Avantians sound stranger all the time!" Luke replied. "Ursus has never abandoned us, so I'll stick with him."

As he took the first mouthful of his stew, thunder rumbled from above. Luke frowned.

"That's odd," he said. "There's no

storm approaching."

Brendan stood up, and pointed.
"Oh yes there is."

Luke saw a small black cloud
floating in the sky. He reached for
his staff and stood beside his father.
"What could it be?"

"Let's investigate," Brendan replied.

They scrambled down the path from
the caves. With a sharp crack, the
cloud parted. Luke grabbed his father's
tunic and tugged him behind a tree.

"There's something inside!" he
gasped.

As they watched, a stone staircase
emerged from the black smoke,
reaching downwards in a spiral. Luke
could feel his father trembling.

"What magic is this?" he asked.

As the steps touched the ground
not far from their tree, Luke saw two

figures emerge from the black smoke.
First came a man wearing a dark
hooded cloak. He carried a staff made
of gnarled wood. This cloaked figure
led a short, fat girl wearing a silly
pointed hat. Dark, lank tresses hung
over her shoulder, and her eyes
squinted into the light. The man
reached the bottom of the steps, then
crouched and laid his hand on the
soil. His face twisted into a sneer.

"It worked!" the man said. "We've reached Seraph."

The girl hopped from foot to foot, giggling. "It's ours!" she said.

"*What's* theirs?" whispered Luke.

Brendan cautiously stepped out from his hiding place. "Come on, son. You know Seraph's first law."

"Welcome to all," Luke replied.

Although Brendan felt uneasy, he nodded. "Let's greet our visitors."

Striding ahead of his son, he approached the man and his girl companion. He held out his fist, ready to touch knuckles in the gesture used by all the people of Seraph.

"Greetings, visitors!" he began. "Welcome to—"

The girl gave a squeal of horror and shot out an arm. A bolt of purple light crackled from her fingertips towards them, and Brendan felt a scorching pain across his hand.

"Get away from us!" the man snarled.

Brendan pulled Luke to safety back behind the tree. "They must have misunderstood," Luke said. When he peered around the trunk once more, the two figures were hurrying away, and the man was pointing towards the distant mountains.

"I don't think they're nice people," Luke muttered. "They seem to be looking for something."

"This doesn't feel good," Brendan said. "We should go back to the caves and warn the rest of the tribe."

Cradling his injured hand, he looked back, but the strangers had vanished. He shuddered. Something evil had arrived in Seraph...

CHAPTER ONE

HOMECOMING

Errinel appeared on the horizon and Tom's heart lifted. He pushed Storm harder, and the black stallion responded with a burst of speed. Tendrils of smoke from several chimneys rose above the familiar houses. Tom couldn't quite believe Avantia was safe again. Sanpao the Pirate King had been banished for good, and his mother Freya and Silver were freed from Tavania.

"How does it feel to be home?" shouted Elenna.

He looked sideways to where she galloped on Blizzard, the beautiful white mare she'd met on their previous Quest.

"It feels great!" Tom replied.

Elenna's wolf, Silver, bounded between the horses, his tongue lolling. Tom looked back over his shoulder. Behind him, on a magnificent chestnut stallion, rode his father Taladon, wearing his shining golden armour. And at his side Freya sat in the saddle of a bay war-horse.

For a long time, he'd never dreamed his mother was alive, let alone that she and his father could be reunited. As Mistress of the Beasts, her Quests had taken her far and wide to battle evil.

Tom felt pride welling up inside him. *We're a family for the first time!*

They slowed to a canter as they passed the outer reaches of Errinel. Tom couldn't wait to see Aunt Maria and Uncle Henry's faces when they clapped eyes on their visitors.

Outside the stables, Tom and the other riders dismounted and tied their horses up.

"I haven't been here for years," said Freya. "But it looks just the same."

Tom led the way to the forge where his uncle worked. Even before they arrived they heard the clang of a hammer. Tom signalled for the others to stay outside and pushed open the door. A blast of heat baked his face, and he saw Uncle Henry bent over an anvil, sweat dripping from his brow. He held a bar of red-hot iron in a pair of tongs. In his other hand he gripped a hammer. With expert strokes, he bent the iron into the shape of a horseshoe. As he dropped the shoe, hissing, into a barrel of water, Tom called out, "Uncle!"

Henry spun around, wiping the sweat from his forehead. His face broke into a broad grin.

"Tom!" he cried. "It's been so long! Is everything all right?"

Tom nodded and clapped his uncle on the shoulder. "Everything's fine. I've brought visitors!" He looked at the door. "Come in, all of you."

As Taladon led Freya inside, Uncle Henry's eyes widened. "It can't...it can't be!"

"It is!" said Freya.

"Maria!" Uncle Henry shouted, dropping the hammer and tearing off the leather apron. He rushed forward, pulling both Freya and Taladon into his huge embrace.

"What is it?" called a woman's voice.

"Come quickly!" Henry shouted.

"I'm making a cherry pie!" Tom's Aunt Maria called back.

"That can wait!" shouted Henry, as Tom and his father began to laugh. They both loved Maria's cherry pie. "You really have to see this!"

Aunt Maria came in, her hands coated in flour. "If the crust burns, I'll hit you with my rolling..." She gasped as her eyes fell on Taladon and Freya. Tears sprang into her eyes as she joined the huddle.

Tom drew back to stand with

Elenna. He knew how hard it must be for her at times like this: her parents were long dead.

"There must be a feast!" Uncle Henry announced. "Let's celebrate the return of my brother and his wife."

Elenna was charged with spreading the news around the village, while Tom and his parents arranged tables

in the main square. Soon families emerged from all the houses carrying platters of food. The owner of the local tavern dragged out a barrel of apple juice. A hog roast turned on a spit and a cauldron of stew bubbled.

Musicians began to play a jig, and Tom was amazed to see his mother and father dancing. Freya was much better, but Taladon made a game effort to keep up with her rapid steps. Silver bounded around Freya's heels.

"Want to try?" asked Elenna, her face flushed.

"Why not?" said Tom. But as he led the way to the dancing area, he noticed a strange blue glow coming from behind the village hall. "Wait a moment," he muttered. "What's that?"

Elenna followed him around behind the bubbling stew pot, to

where a familiar figure was dusting off his brown travelling cloak.

Tom's face broke into a smile. "Aduro! What are you doing here?"

The wizard threw up his hands. "I need to talk with..." He tailed off as a puppy rounded the side of the building, pursued by two small children. "You don't think I'd miss the celebration, do you?" he continued, darting a nervous glance at the children. "Now show me the way to some food. I'm starving!"

As Tom led his wizard friend back to the party, he wondered why Aduro had really come. Aduro placed an arm over his and Elenna's shoulders. "Best keep my identity a secret, I think. We don't want people worrying about a wizard in their midst."

Tom nodded. "Of course. Though

Father might need a bit of magic to help with his dancing."

Elenna and Aduro laughed as they mingled with the crowd.

"Who's this?" said Uncle Henry, appearing before them, arm in arm with Aunt Maria.

"An old friend from the palace," said Elenna quickly. "Just passing through."

After they'd settled Aduro down with some food, Elenna went to get more wood for the giant bonfire. Tom was wondering whether to go for a second helping of roasted meat, when he noticed that Aduro had barely touched a morsel on his plate.

"Something's wrong, isn't it?" he asked.

Aduro looked down at him gravely. "Sorry to spoil the party," he said, "but can you fetch Taladon and Freya? Elenna too. I'll wait by the stables."

Tom felt a ball of dread gather in his gut. He pushed through the whirling bodies of the dancers until he found his parents. "I need to talk with you," he said. They heard the seriousness in his tone, because they stopped dancing and followed wordlessly. He found Elenna feeding a large piece of pork to Silver, and gestured for her to come too.

Back near the stables, Aduro stood stroking Storm's nose. He peered past them, nervously. "I'm afraid I haven't come here for the celebrations," he said. "Word has reached me of grave events."

"What is it?" asked Taladon.

"Our oldest enemy," said Aduro.

"Malvel?" Tom breathed.

The wizard nodded. "You know that he escaped when the prison was destroyed. Well, I hoped that would be the last we'd see of him."

"No chance," said Elenna.

"He's been spotted near the palace," Aduro went on. "Tom and Elenna must return to the city as soon as possible. The King needs them!"

CHAPTER TWO

THE WARLOCK'S STAFF

"I'll come too!" said Taladon.

"And me," said Freya.

Aduro shook his head. "That won't be possible. The land of Gwildor has sent a message for help. Freya must fulfil her duty as their Mistress of the Beasts. I fear Taladon is needed there, too."

Taladon smiled. "I trust Tom to handle whatever peril Avantia faces."

"Gwildor is many days' travel," said Freya. "We must leave at once."

"No matter," said Aduro. He held up his hand, and closed his eyes. The ground began to shake, and Storm whinnied. A few paces away, the hard earth broke open. Tom's heartbeat quickened when the Tree of Being sprouted from the soil, rising up high above them.

"It's all right, boy," he muttered to his stallion.

"The portal in the tree will take you to Gwildor," said Aduro.

The sounds of the feast carried over to them and Tom realised the villagers were all too busy dancing and singing to notice a new tree on the edge of Errinel. Fetching their horses, Taladon and Freya approached the magical trunk.

A section of the bark had already disappeared, leaving a roughly hewn archway with only blackness beyond.

Freya gave Tom a swift embrace.

"Goodbye, son," she said sadly. "Keep Avantia safe. We'll be together again soon."

"Good luck," Tom replied. He'd only just found his mother and now they were to be parted again.

Taladon went first, after slapping Tom on the shoulder. He melted into the portal, and Freya followed. Silver barked, as though bidding them farewell. Then the doorway swallowed them up. The arch rippled as they vanished. With a sound of rustling leaves the trunk disappeared back into the ground.

Tom told himself to be strong.

"They'll be all right," whispered Elenna.

"I didn't want to snatch them away so soon," said Aduro, "but we can't wait any longer. My magic can take us to the palace. Fetch Storm."

As Tom led them to the stable and untied his faithful stallion, he heard Elenna ask, "What about Blizzard?"

"She'll be safer here," said Aduro. Silver whined. "Looks like someone doesn't want to be left behind, though. Are you ready?"

"Ready!" Tom and Elenna replied.

Aduro waved his hand. Tom felt dizzy for a moment as blue light climbed around them. In a flash, Errinel vanished and the distant music ceased.

Where am I? In the darkness, Tom smelled burning.

"No!" cried Aduro, taking a lantern down from the wall. "We're too late."

"What is it?" asked Elenna.

Tom realised they were beside the palace armoury, but the air was thick with smoke. The two great iron-studded doors of the arms room lay smashed off their hinges, and one was cracked down the centre.

"Quick!" said Tom. "Someone might be hurt. We must help."

He rushed into the chamber, with Aduro and Elenna close behind.

A shadow moved in the smoke, and Tom's hand reached for his sword-hilt. The Master of Arms staggered out from the smoke-filled armoury, one hand clutching his bleeding temple. Tom went to support him.

"I don't know what happened!" the man cried.

Aduro's face went deathly pale. "Malvel," he breathed. "This could only be his work. I've been so stupid!"

"Can you make it to the infirmary?" Tom asked the Master of Arms.

The man nodded, and stumbled off.

"What's going on?" asked Elenna.

Aduro walked across the chamber. Tom went after him, and saw the wizard reach for the wall. He inserted his index finger between two stones, where the mortar had crumbled away. Squinting with concentration, he pulled down hard on something. Tom heard a click, followed by a thunk. The wall opened like a narrow door. Aduro peered inside, then let out a groan and fell to his knees. "It's gone!"

Tom looked past him. Inside was a small chamber containing nothing but a red velvet cushion on a low altar. "What's gone?" he asked. He'd never seen this hidden chamber before.

"The Warlock's Staff," Aduro said weakly. "Malvel must have sent a false message from Gwildor to make me leave. It gave him time to steal it."

Aduro climbed slowly to his feet. Elenna put a hand on the wizard's

arm. "The kingdom has lost other things: golden armour, a golden cup, the Book of Life… We'll find this Staff and bring it back."

Aduro reached for the wall to steady himself, his skin grey. "You don't understand. The Warlock's Staff is different. It was cut from the Tree of Being, and gives a fearful power to whoever wields it."

Aduro looks years older, Tom thought.

"What sort of power?" he asked.

"The power to enter the Realm of Seraph," said the wizard. "And worse. If Malvel manages to burn the staff in Seraph's Eternal Flame, he will be invincible. He'll be able to travel between worlds at will. He'll rule over each and every kingdom with unstoppable magic."

Tom and Elenna exchanged panicked glances.

"Where is this Realm of Seraph?" Elenna asked. "We'll go there and stop Malvel."

"Seraph floats above Avantia," said the wizard. "It's a perfect world where fruit tastes sweeter and water sparkles like diamonds; where no evil is done. There aren't even any Beasts there – good or bad."

"Why haven't you mentioned it

before?" asked Tom.

Aduro's knees buckled and he almost fell. Tom rushed forward and caught him. "Seraph is a secret passed from one wizard to the next," said their friend. "We swear an oath never to speak of it. The risk is too great if a force for evil wants to burn the Staff. Now all is lost."

The wizard leant heavily on his shoulders. "Don't worry," Tom said. "Elenna and I will make sure Malvel doesn't succeed."

Aduro shook his head, his eyes watery and his skin furrowed with wrinkles. "I can't let you," he gasped. "It's too dangerous. Too much to ask. I'm too…weak."

Under his robes, Aduro's limbs felt stick-thin. *Something's not right here*, Tom thought. *Why is he so weak?*

"Aduro!" said Elenna. "What's happening to you?"

The wizard turned to look at Tom, his mouth turned down. His skin looked papery. "Without the staff in its rightful place, my life is over," he said.

"What?" Tom gasped. "Why didn't you say?"

Aduro's voice came out as barely a croak. "...been that way since the first wizard," he said. He gripped Tom's forearm with clawed fingers. "Farewell, Tom. Unless you get the Staff back, I leave you for ever..."

With a sigh as though Aduro was breathing his last breath, Tom felt the body under the robes disappear. The wizard's cloak and hat fell to the ground empty.

Aduro had vanished.

CHAPTER THREE

STAIRWAY TO ANOTHER WORLD

Tom stared at the crumpled clothes on the floor of the armoury.

"It can't be," said Elenna, her voice quavering.

Tom swallowed. "He's gone. You heard what he said. Without the Staff, he's…" He couldn't say the word *dead*, but grief washed over him. The wizard who'd steered them through so many Quests...could he really have gone?

"What do we do now?" asked Elenna, her eyes brimming with tears.

Tom clenched his fists. "We do exactly what he told us not to," he said. "We travel to Seraph. We find Malvel, and we make him pay for what he's done."

"Perhaps if we find the Staff, Aduro will come back," said Elenna.

Tom nodded. "We have to stop Malvel burning the Staff."

Elenna crouched beside the garments and began to scoop them up tenderly. "Wait a moment!" she said. "What's this? Aduro's left us something!"

From beneath the robe, she pulled out a roll of linen, tied with leather cords.

Tom managed to smile at Aduro's final act of kindness. "He must have used the last of his magic," he said. "What's inside?"

He crouched beside Elenna and helped her un-knot the bindings. She rolled out the linen to reveal...

"Six small objects," she murmured.

"Tokens!" Tom realised. "He's given us six pieces of magic."

Elenna picked up a small dagger, a little longer than Tom's hand, with a glass blade. There was a vial too, filled with blue liquid.

Poison, perhaps? thought Tom, placing it down carefully beside what looked like a miniature harp.

"Don't we normally get the tokens *after* defeating the Beasts?" asked Elenna.

Tom shrugged. "Aduro said there

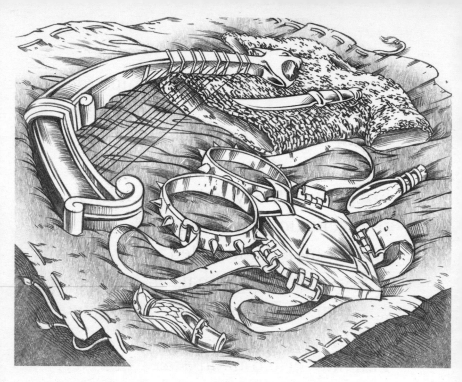

weren't any Beasts in Seraph. Unless
Aduro thinks Beasts are going to
invade the kingdom. Even then,
I don't see what use a musical
instrument will be against Malvel's
magic."

The other items were stranger still.
A vest of gossamer-thin chain mail,
which weighed next to nothing. A
strange harness made from leather

44

straps. And finally, carved from jade, an object in the shape of a bird, the size of his thumb with two holes.

"It's a whistle!" said Elenna, bringing it slowly to her lips. When she blew, no sound emerged, but Silver howled and rolled over.

"Perhaps only animals can hear it," Tom said. He gathered up the objects and retied the cords of the bag. Elenna wiped a hand across her face.

"None of this is any use at all," she said, "unless we can actually get to Seraph. What did Aduro say – it's *above* Avantia?"

"Perhaps Malvel left some clue when he was here," Tom said. He walked back to the exposed secret hatch in the wall.

Tom leant in and pulled away the cushion. A crack ran through the stone tabletop. Tom gripped the edge, and pulled. With a grinding sound, the tabletop shifted a little.

"I think I've found something," he muttered. "Come and help me."

Elenna rushed to his side, and together they took an edge of the table's surface, and heaved. It scraped and groaned, then toppled onto the ground, smashing into several chunks. A smell of stale air rose through the chamber.

Tom peered into the hollow altar table. A flight of steps descended into the bowels of Avantia. After half a dozen of them, blackness swallowed up the secret stairwell.

"As I thought. It's a passage!"

"It must lead to Seraph!" Elenna said.

As soon as the words had left her

mouth, the walls of the chamber trembled, and dust and chips of stone scattered on the floor. The stairwell itself began to shift. The steps rose up from the darkness towards Tom.

"Get out of the way!" he shouted over the roar.

He and Elenna staggered backwards as the stairs twisted upwards like a corkscrew from the altar table, then smashed through the roof. Great chunks of masonry collapsed around them, and daylight flooded in. The stairs continued to grow, shooting straight up into the sky, climbing to an impossible height through the clouds.

"Is that where we're meant to go?" asked Elenna, looking up.

"It must be," Tom replied. He gripped his shield firmly and put his

foot on the first step.

"Wait," said Elenna. "What about the animals?"

"You're right!" Tom closed his eyes, concentrating on the power of Kaymon's diamond in his belt. It gave him the ability to separate his shadow from his body. He watched the dark shape race from the chamber, turning to give him a thumbs up before disappearing down the main stairs. *Go to the stables to fetch Storm and Silver*, he silently ordered his shadow.

Soon he heard the rattle of Storm's hooves on the stairs, and both animals burst into the chamber. Silver's ears were pricked up.

Tom's shadow seeped back into him.

"That was quick!" said Elenna.

"Since I got the belt back from
Sanpao the Pirate King, it seems
more powerful than ever," said Tom.

He took hold of Storm's reins, and
led him onto the first of the steps.
Elenna followed behind him, with
Silver pressed close to her legs. The
four of them climbed. Beneath them,
Tom saw the palace towers.
Fortunately, the market in the
courtyard below was so busy that no
one glanced up to see them climbing
into the sky.

Wind whipped at their clothes as
they mounted higher. Dizziness
swept over Tom when he noticed the
bottom steps had started to vanish.
"There's nothing supporting us but
magic," he said. "Let's hope Seraph's
not far!"

Soon the people in the palace

grounds were tiny as ants. Faces turned up to them as groups gathered and pointed. Tom and Elenna passed through the first shreds of cloud, and the ground beneath them disappeared completely. They broke out into a perfect, clear blue sky. The air was icy cold, and Tom saw Elenna's lips had turned almost purple. Storm's legs were trembling with the climb.

Suddenly they reached the top of the steps. Another set of stairs descended down, as though they'd reached the pinnacle of some enormous mountain. Hugging himself to keep warm, Tom began the descent. As soon as his foot lighted on the first step, a shiver of warmth trickled along his limbs. "Did you feel that?" he asked Elenna.

She nodded. "It must be some sort of magic."

They passed back through the cloud cover, and out of the cold. As they emerged, the castle had vanished and the landscape was completely different.

"Seraph!" Elenna gasped.

Tom stared at the new kingdom. Wild forests lay dotted among fields of brilliant green, and lakes glittered gold in the sunlight. In the distance, white mountains thrust jagged peaks into the sky and in the opposite direction an ocean spread as far as Tom could see.

"It's beautiful!" he said, his heart thumping.

Silver howled in agreement and rushed on ahead. Elenna quickened her steps too, while Tom led Storm.

Soon they'd reached the bottom. They found themselves in a beautiful valley, sparsely scattered with fruit trees. A river gurgled from a pass at the far end, and shallow rocky ridges lined each side. The air smelled of blossom.

Tom saw a narrow track leading to a river valley. "Come on, perhaps Malvel went this way."

They scrambled onto Storm's saddle, and Silver ran alongside. As they climbed, doubts clouded Tom's heart. "I wish we had a map," he murmured.

Silver suddenly stopped, ears flattened. "He's sensed something," Elenna said.

For a moment, Tom could see nothing on the path ahead. But then the shape of a horse appeared on the

horizon, coming out of the sun. He
squinted, and made out a rider.

"Thank goodness!" he said.
"Perhaps this person can help us find
Malvel."

But as the stranger drew nearer,
Tom saw that it wasn't a horse at all.
Not *just* a horse, anyway.

Although the creature had the body of a black stallion like Storm, wings sprouted from either flank. Foam fell from the creature's fangs and a twisted horn jutted from its forehead.

"It's some kind of unicorn!" gasped Elenna.

But Tom wasn't looking at the steed anymore. He fixed his attention on the rider.

Even if the pointed witch's hat hadn't given away her identity, the giggle that came from her throat was more than enough.

"Petra!" Tom yelled.

CHAPTER FOUR

AN OLD ENEMY

Tom drew his sword, but Petra slipped from the unicorn's saddle when she was still ten paces away. She danced from foot to foot. The last time Tom had seen Malvel's minion was during his Quest to fight Mortaxe the Skeleton Warrior, but she'd escaped before he could capture her.

"Greetings, old friends!' she called.

"How good of you to join us."

"Where's Malvel?" asked Tom.

"Waiting for you!" laughed Petra. "He's got something you want, I believe."

"The Warlock's Staff belongs in Avantia!" Tom said.

Petra stroked the black unicorn's mane, and it tossed its head, baring its yellow fangs. "It belongs in the Eternal Flame," she snapped. "When we've burned the staff, we'll have power over all kingdoms."

Tom's hand tightened on the sword hilt. "While there's blood in my veins, I'll never let that happen," he said.

Petra threw back her head and cackled. "You're alone, Tom. No wizard to help you." She pulled out a wand, aiming it at Tom.

"Oh no, you don't!" he called. He quickly slung his shield across his front, but as Petra sent out a bolt of light he felt his throat tighten, as though he was being strangled.

"Help…" Choking, he fell to his knees.

Elenna jumped down from the saddle, and strung an arrow to her bow. She trained it on the witch.

"Let him go!" she shouted.

Petra twitched her wand, and the pressure on Tom's neck disappeared.

"Learned a few new tricks, have you?" he asked, massaging his bruised skin.

"Here's another!" she said. The black unicorn spread his wings and bounded forward, as high as Storm's head. Tom just had time to raise his shield as the creature's front hooves pounded into the wood, jolting his shoulder. Storm whinnied in panic and reared up.

"Trample him to dust, Noctus!" Petra giggled.

Tom stood in front of Storm as the unicorn attacked again. He stabbed upwards with his sword, but only managed to strike sparks on the creature's hooves.

Noctus landed a few paces away, snorting in anger. His wild eyes swivelled to Elenna.

"Look out!" said Tom.

The snarling unicorn lowered his head and charged. Elenna had barely lifted her bow when Noctus struck. His horn ripped through the tunic at her side. Elenna cried out in pain as she slammed into the ground, gasping for breath.

"Finish her!" shouted Petra.

Noctus stamped the ground, and lowered his deadly horn for the killing blow. Tom leapt forwards but he knew he wasn't quick enough. As Noctus galloped towards Elenna, Silver leapt up with a growl, and sunk his teeth into the top of the unicorn's rear leg. It was enough to slow the evil creature, and while he

bucked and thrashed to shake the
brave wolf loose, Tom helped Elenna
to her feet. He checked her side for
a wound.

"It's only a graze," she said bravely.

Noctus sent Silver tumbling, and
retreated at a canter to Petra's side.
Petra cast her wand over the
teeth-marks on the unicorn's side,

healing them instantly.

"It'll take more than your filthy
unicorn to scare us," said Elenna,
her face pale.

"Then it's lucky I have this," said
Petra. She slipped her spare hand
inside her robe. When she pulled it
out again, she clutched a deadly short
dagger, its blade glowing red hot like

a poker left in a fire. Smoke swirled around her wrist. Silver whined with unease, his hackles rising, and Noctus bared his fangs.

"Malvel wanted to play with you both a little," said Petra, her lank hair falling over her face. "But I don't see any reason not to kill you now."

Tom brandished his sword. "I'd like to see you try," he said. Beside him, he saw Elenna put two arrows across her bowstring at the same time.

"Let's see how good your magic is," she said.

Noctus retreated a few steps and Petra leapt forward with a hiss, casting a bolt of green energy from her wand. Tom deflected it with his shield, but the blow sent him stumbling backwards into Storm. Elenna loosed her arrows, and Petra

leapt nimbly aside, then thrust her
dagger. Tom jumped up, slashing up
with his sword. The dagger spun
from Petra's hand and landed on the
ground behind her. As she ran for it,
Elenna used her bow to hook the
witch's foot. Her wand snapped in
two as she hit the dirt. Petra
scrambled up with a cry of anger,
but as she did, another object fell
from her tunic.

Elenna lunged and snatched it up
at the same time as Petra seized her
dagger once more. She faced them
with the wand hanging uselessly in
one hand.

"A scroll!" said Elenna.

"That's mine!" Petra snapped.

"It's over!" said Tom, now back
on his feet and advancing with his
sword.

Petra's face twitched with indecision. She wasn't giggling any more.

"Give yourself up," Elenna panted.

"Never!" said Petra. She scurried back to Noctus's side, and hauled herself clumsily into the saddle. "Take me back to Malvel!" she ordered.

The black creature lifted her head and spread ash-coloured wings. With three strong wing-beats she was airborne, and sweeping away above them.

"Where did you get that Beast?" Elenna shouted.

Petra looked down, grinning cruelly. "Haven't you worked it out yet?" she yelled back. "We *corrupted* it! We're creating all the Beasts in Seraph. See for yourself!"

She dropped the broken wand and waved a hand in the air. A cloud formed between them as she rode away.

CHAPTER FIVE

VICTIMS OF MALVEL

Tom and Elenna looked into the cloud and saw a vision forming. A brown bear sat beside a tree, fishing sticky honey from a fallen beehive with his paw. Suddenly its body went rigid, and its lips drew back to reveal sharp teeth, growing by the moment.

"It's changing!" said Elenna. "It must be Petra's magic!"

The bear rolled onto its back, growling in pain. Its body swelled and orange spikes pushed outwards through its skin. Tom watched in horror as its snout grew longer and its ears wider, flickering to take in any sound. The Beast lumbered to its feet and roared, shaking the leaves of the tree. Then, with curled claws as big as scythes, it tore the bark away in huge shards.

Tom shuddered at the thought of facing this terrible creature.

As the vision faded, he saw the escaping witch was no more than a dot in the sky.

"She's going to join Malvel," said Elenna.

"That's what we have to do too," said Tom, gripping Storm's reins. "Let's see what Petra left behind."

"Good idea," said Elenna. She unfurled the linen scroll that Petra had dropped, and laid it over the ground, still spotted with Noctus's blood. Silver sniffed at it unsurely.

"It's a map!" Tom said. He tried to contain his rising excitement as he scanned the surface. The tapestry showed the whole kingdom of Seraph, including valleys, ridges, lakes, villages and mountains. The kingdom was shaped like a long tongue of land, with the sea on either side. Tom's eyes were immediately drawn to a small image of a flame in the north of the kingdom, on top of a tall mountain lined with dangerous-looking crags. Script spelled out: *The Eternal Flame of Seraph.*

"It's many days' travel," said Tom. "There's no time to lose."

They were in the south of the kingdom at the moment, Tom realised, where the fruit valley was marked, and a thin silvery thread on the map glinted in the sunlight. Tom hadn't seen it until that moment. He traced it with his finger to a forest. A tiny picture of a bear appeared, and beneath it was written Ursus.

"Ursus must be the name of the Bear-Beast," said Elenna.

"We have to put that right," said Tom. "Those Beasts could attack anyone in Seraph."

"And what about the Warlock's Staff?" Elenna asked. "That's our only hope of bringing Aduro back to life."

"Malvel has that, too. Come on. We have to get after him. Let's ride!"

They set off at a gallop towards the forest on the east coast of the kingdom. The air smelled crisp and clean; the trees were straight and tall, and their leaves seemed almost to glow in the sunlight. But the going was tough, with thick vines coating the forest floor, and tangling Storm's hooves. Tom had to pick a careful path between the tightly-packed trees. As Tom brushed past a

low-hanging branch, he pushed
it aside with his hand.

"Wait a moment!" he said.

He rode over to where a glossy pear
hung from a branch. They hadn't
eaten since arriving in the kingdom.
Slowly he reached out and plucked
the fruit. With his stomach growling,
he sank his teeth into the juicy flesh,
savouring the sweet flavour. He
handed another back to Elenna.

"We should eat while we can,"
he told her.

"It's delicious!" she said, tucking in.

Tom wiped the sticky juice from his
hands and checked the map. "Ursus
should be around here somewhere."

Silver growled, flattening his ears.

"What is it, boy?" asked Elenna.

Tom glanced up to the sky, in case
Petra decided to make a reappearance

on Noctus. Silver nosed ahead through the undergrowth. Tom urged Storm at a slow trot after the wolf. They emerged into a clearing, with an ivy-clad and moss-covered rockface ahead of them. Several dark caves opened into the stone wall.

"Perhaps this is Ursus's lair," said Tom, drawing his sword.

"I don't think so," said Elenna. "Look." She pointed at one of the distant cave mouths, and Tom saw fish being smoked over a gentle fire, and animal furs hanging up to dry. "I think people live here."

Storm neighed loudly, and sure enough, Tom and Elenna heard voices. A moment later, a group of four – two men, one young and one old, and a woman and a little girl – peered out from the far cave. They were dressed in simple animal skins, and when they saw Tom and Elenna they clutched each other.

"They're back!" said the younger man. "The man and the girl!"

They think we're Malvel and Petra, Tom realised. He quickly put his sword away, and held up both arms. "We mean you no harm," he called. "We're new to this kingdom."

The older man peered closer. "It's not them. That's a boy, and the girl is not wearing a hat."

The tribes-people cautiously stepped into the open. They carried no weapons, Tom noticed. When they were just a few paces away, he said, "I think you mistook us for our enemies, Malvel and Petra. They must have been this way already."

"Please, leave us," said the old

man. "We don't want any trouble."

Tom noticed that the little girl
cowering at her mother's side had a
nasty gouge on her cheek. Also, the
young man's animal fur had been
shredded at the bottom. *Almost like*

claw marks, Tom thought. Elenna must have seen too, because she spoke up first.

"Has a bear been here?" she asked.

The older man laughed bitterly. "Not just any bear," he said. "Ursus the Clawed Roar!"

"Don't talk to them, Brendan," said the woman. "You don't know who they are."

"He sounds frightening," said Elenna.

"He never used to be," said the little girl. "We used to play music to him. He used to look after us. All the forest people. But today..." Her words trailed off.

"Today he tore into the settlement," said the man called Brendan. "He'd changed almost beyond recognition. He'd become a huge bear with a spiked pelt and the strangest, curling claws. He attacked people! He rampaged through the campfires and hammocks, knocking down huts and tearing up crops. He's gone again, thank goodness but" – he peered into the forest beyond – "we don't know when he might come back."

"We don't know what made him change," chipped in Luke. His eyes narrowed. "It happened when the strangers came."

Tom looked at the four sad, scared faces below him. "It was people from my world who brought this misery," he said. "And I give you my promise we'll put it right."

CHAPTER SIX

THE CLAWED ROAR

"Malvel wants to get to the Eternal Flame," said Elenna. "And we're the only ones who can stop him."

"The Eternal Flame is deadly," said the young man. "No one has ever seen it and returned alive."

Just then, Tom's stomach growled again.

"You're hungry," said the little girl. "Come and eat with us."

"We can't—" Tom began to protest, but the girl's mother cut him off.

"Please," she said. "We wouldn't be true people of Seraph if we didn't treat our visitors with kindness."

"We have to eat," Elenna whispered to Tom. "All we've had is that fruit. How can we complete a Quest if we're starving?"

The young man stepped forward and held out his fist. Tom looked at it blankly.

"This is how we greet friends in Seraph," said the woman.

"Oh!" said Tom. He climbed down from Storm's saddle, and held out his own hand in the same way. They touched knuckles and Luke smiled. Brendan did the same. As he did so, he held up his other hand, which was bandaged.

"Your enemy Malvel gave me this,"
he said.

Tom raised his eyebrows. "That's
the type of thing he does."

They went to sit by the fire. Myra
played with Silver in the grass, while
Greta offered Tom and Elenna a plate
of the smoked fish and bread.

As they were halfway through their
second helping, Brendan took out
a set of pipes and began blowing a
tune. Luke accompanied him on a set
of skin drums. It made Tom think of
Myra's words about playing music to

the bear, and one of the tokens
wrapped up in Storm's saddle bag.
He leant over to Elenna. "Do you
think the miniature harp might help
us against Ursus?" he said.

"How would a pretty little harp
help to defeat a Beast?" she asked.

Tom wasn't sure, but he knew for
certain that he didn't want to kill the
Beast. It wasn't Ursus's fault that he'd
turned bad; the blame lay squarely at
Malvel's feet.

He finished his plate, and set it
down. "Thank you for your
hospitality," he said, "but we must
keep moving. Can you tell us where
we can find Ursus?"

Brendan nodded gravely. "He used
to dwell by the Great Waterfall," he
said, pointing past the cave entrances.
"You follow the stream. But be

warned, Ursus's sense of smell is second to none."

"He'll pick up the scent of anyone approaching, and now he's dangerous!" put in Luke. "You must do what you can to disguise yourselves."

"I know just the thing," said Greta. She stood up and went to the edge of the clearing, scooping something up with her hands. When she returned Tom saw what she was carrying.

"Rabbit droppings?" he said, frowning.

"It's just the thing," said Greta. She rubbed them together in her hands, and began to smear them over Tom's clothes. He tried not to flinch.

"You too!" he said to Elenna, grimacing.

"Do I have to?" she said uneasily.

She looked sick as she covered herself in squashed-up droppings.

When they had finished, Silver sniffed uncertainly at Elenna, and Myra laughed.

"I think you smell better now!"

"Thanks," said Tom, taking Storm's reins. He led them to the edge of the clearing.

"It's not far to the stream," said Brendan. "And remember, be careful. Ursus is not to be trifled with."

Tom held out his hand, and they bumped knuckles again. "Thank you for trusting us," he said. "I won't let you down."

He turned into the forest. It wasn't long before the trees swallowed up all the light. Something dropped from the tree above.

"What was that?" Elenna asked.

As she stood, Tom saw a spider the size of his hand sitting on her shoulder, crawling towards her neck. He quickly brushed it off with his shield.

"Thanks!" she said.

All around them, the jungle rustled with low noises and the sound of scurrying. A rat ran over Tom's feet. "We should press on quickly," he said.

They found the stream, and followed it up towards its source. Snakes nosed through the undergrowth, hissing menacingly. Silver chased some off.

"I hear something!" said Elenna. Standing still for a moment, Tom picked out the faint crash of water.

"It must be the waterfall!" he said, quickening his steps over wet rocks, and through muddy puddles.

They emerged into a clearing.
A huge cascade broke over the craggy
cliff-face, thundering into a crystal-
clear pool below. Small rainbows
arced through the water and mist
bathed Tom's cheeks, cooling him.

"It's beautiful!" said Elenna.

Tom led Storm by the reins around
the edge of the pool towards the
white shower of water. Silver leapt
up with excitement.

"I think he wants to jump in," said
Elenna, grinning broadly.

When they were level with the
waterfall, Tom couldn't help himself.
It looks so cool and refreshing. He leaned
out from the bank to place his hand
in the torrent. Then he glimpsed
something behind the moving sheet
of water – something truly terrifying.

A huge roar filled the air as a set
of jaws opened wide, exposing
glistening red gums and piercing
fangs. A giant bear sat on the rocks
behind the waterfall, his huge flanks
rising and falling.

Ursus!

CHAPTER SEVEN

THE SCENT OF PREY

"Get out of here!" Tom cried, leaping
to his feet and running towards a
large boulder higher up the slope.
He and Elenna crept behind it with
Storm and Silver following. The
ground was loose underfoot,
covered in gravel and pebbles.

When Tom and his companions
were safely out of sight, he and

Elenna peered over the top. Ursus had emerged from behind the waterfall and was gazing around, roaring with anger. But they'd been too quick for the lumbering Beast.

He has no idea where we're hiding, thought Tom.

He shuddered. He couldn't imagine how the cave people might ever have lived side by side with such a creature. Ursus was three times the size of a fully-grown bear, his body as big as a cart. His brown pelt wasn't slick and healthy, but looked torn away in patches, with orange spikes pushing through, and glowing as though the Beast was lit by fire from inside. His claws were as long as Tom's sword. His ears quivered, alert for any sound. His nostrils flared as he sniffed the air.

Tom felt the loose pebbles shift

beneath his feet and caught himself against the rock. He froze, breath caught in his throat, as several small stones clattered down to where Ursus sat. The Beast's ears twitched. He lifted his massive snout, and Tom caught sight of dagger-like teeth as the Beast's black lips drew back. Ursus sniffed, turned his head, and sniffed again.

Can he smell us, Tom wondered, *despite the droppings?* If only he hadn't put his hand in that waterfall! The flesh of his arm was washed clean, allowing his scent to escape.

Tom glanced at Elenna, and saw her watching the bear. He tried to calm his breathing, but his heart was pounding in his chest.

Elenna mouthed a question: "What do we do?"

Tom leant across and slipped his

hand silently into Storm's saddle bag. He rooted around until his hand fell on the miniature harp.

What had the little girl said? *We used to play music to him…* Tom gazed at the token now. Aduro couldn't have had any idea what Beasts Malvel would create in Seraph. It was down to Tom to work out which token to use against which Beast. *I have no idea if this will work against Ursus*, he thought, *but it's the only option I have.* For the first time in his life, he was facing a Quest without any of the good wizard's wise words. *I'll do this for Aduro. And I'll bring my old friend back to life!*

There was a sudden roar of defiance. Tom slipped his hand out of the saddle bag – the tokens would have to wait. He peered over the rock

to check what Ursus was doing.
Elenna did the same, but
overbalanced slightly.

Ursus's head snapped round, his
ears alert. The Beast looked up,
sniffing the air, and Tom looked right
into his eyes. Like his spikes and
claws, they were red as burning coals
and seemed to burn Tom's skin with
hatred.

Malvel created that hate, Tom thought.

Ursus roared, and the sound echoed
through the forest. The Beast
scrambled onto all fours and began
to climb towards them on muscular
legs, claws gripping the cliff face with
surprising agility.

"Stand back!" Tom shouted to
Elenna, fingers scrabbling at his belt.
"I have a plan."

He detached the purple jewel, won

from Sting the Scorpion Man, and held it over the boulder. A saw-blade of purple light erupted from the jewel, slicing into the solid rock to create a rock fall.

"Good thinking," said Elenna. "I'll get the animals to safety."

She hastily led Storm and Silver back down towards the base of the waterfall, safely out of the way. Tom's hand trembled as he forced the jewel to keep sending out its magic, destroying the huge rock. Shards exploded from the boulder, showering the Beast as it climbed. A large chunk slammed into his chest, and knocked the giant bear into the water below. Ursus shook his head and bellowed in defiance, then started to climb again.

The harp! Tom realised it was still

in Storm's saddle bag. He clambered
down towards Elenna and the
animals, now at the forest edge
again. But Ursus was aware of his
every move. As Tom joined the
others, the bear plunged into the
waterfall pool, sending out a huge
wave of water. He swam across with
powerful strokes. In moments, he
would be upon them.

Tom started hacking through the forest vines with his blade to clear a path of escape. If he could just get the others out of the way, he could take the token and face the Beast.

"Quickly, Tom!" Elenna called.

Finally, he found a forest path. "This way!" he shouted. He let Elenna and Silver run ahead, but then he heard a panicked whinnying from Storm. Looking back, he saw Storm thrashing violently, his hooves desperately tangled in ivy that carpeted the forest floor. He was trapped!

Ursus was closing on the stallion with heavy footsteps, his fur dripping and the spikes over his body pulsing orange with every step. His nostrils flared with hatred.

"I have to help Storm," Tom called

to Elenna. He ran back towards
his faithful stallion.

As the Beast paced closer, Tom
hacked at the knotted vines
entangling his horse's legs. He sliced
the last one free, just as the Beast's
shadow lunged towards him.

"Watch out, Tom!" called Elenna.

But it was too late.

CHAPTER EIGHT

CLAWS OF THE BEAST

Tom ducked as Ursus's claws sliced the air above his head, and he rolled across the ground. He leapt to his feet and just had time to slip his hand inside Storm's saddle bag to retrieve the harp.

"Go, boy!" Tom called. "Get out of here." Relief rushed over him as Storm galloped to safety.

The giant bear rose up onto his legs, spreading his front paws wide, and bellowed with fury. He looked down at Tom, opening his saliva-stringed mouth. Stinking breath flooded over him, but Tom caught a glimpse of pain in the Beast's eyes.

He didn't choose to be like this, he thought.

Ursus lunged and snapped his powerful jaws, but Tom smashed the Beast's muzzle with his shield. Giving a growl of fury, Ursus swung his paws, one after the other, like giant scythes. Tom heard the claws whistle past his head.

An arrow thwacked into the tree beside Ursus. He brought a mighty paw down, crushing the shaft like a twig.

"You didn't think I'd leave you to it, did you?" called a voice.

It was Elenna! She shot again, this time into a branch near Ursus's head. Tom could see she wasn't trying to hit the Beast, only to distract him. Ursus snatched this second arrow in his jaws and chewed it into splinters.

As Elenna tried to string another arrow, Ursus bounded towards her, crushing plants beneath him. His mouth frothed with foam and his orange eyes blazed. With a swipe of his claws, he sent the bow spinning from her hands. Elenna dived aside as the Beast pounced, trying to flatten her beneath his massive torso. She darted off behind a nearby tree, pushing herself up against the trunk out of sight.

Ursus found the bow, and crunched it in his jaws. Now Elenna was defenceless!

The Beast sniffed the air, searching

for his prey, then padded closer to the tree where Elenna hid. Tom saw her reach down and take out Petra's dagger from her ankle strap. How was that going to help her against a Beast the size of Ursus? It might give Elenna a few extra moments, but that would be all.

Tom pulled the tiny harp from his tunic. It was worth a try. *I'm putting my faith in you, Aduro*, he thought grimly. The wizard must have given Tom these tokens for a reason.

He plucked a note on the instrument, and Ursus's head jerked around to the sound. Tom strummed once more, this time adding two more notes. His Aunt Maria had played a lyre, which was similar, so Tom quickly managed a simple, repetitive tune. Ursus growled and stalked towards him, but the orange embers of his eyes had faded to dull yellow.

"It's working!" Elenna called over. "Keep playing."

Ursus was just a few paces from Tom now, but he was breathing softly. The Beast lay down in the ferns and moss, his eyelids sagging closed. Tom's heart lifted. Could it really be this easy…? Perhaps this was the key to using the tokens – to trust them, even if they didn't look as though they could do much.

A sudden clap of thunder passed over them, shaking the trees and breaking the charm. It was followed by a cackle of laughter Tom would recognise anywhere. *Malvel!*

Ursus staggered up, his eyes wide and raging again. With a snap of his jaws, he closed his teeth over the harp and tried to tug it away. Tom held on, until with a succession of loud twangs, Ursus's sharp teeth cut though the strings. One of them lashed Tom's hand, cutting into the flesh. He fell back with a pained cry.

As Ursus loomed over him, Silver darted between the Beast's legs, snapping at his belly. With a series

of swipes, Ursus tried to claw at the wolf, and missed. Silver twisted away. Ursus almost toppled, trying to snatch at him.

Tom felt a hand beneath his armpit, and turned to see Elenna helping him to his feet. His hand was dripping blood where the harp string had cut him.

"Your bow…" he began.

"Find me a bamboo shoot," she said. "I've got an idea."

Tom drew his sword and quickly sliced down a bamboo, throwing it to Elenna. Silver was still keeping Ursus busy, out-manoeuvring the Beast near the edge of the water pool.

"Whatever you're planning, you'd better do it fast," said Tom. "I don't know how much longer Silver can distract the Beast!"

Elenna used her hunting dagger

and put notches in the two ends of the bamboo, then strung the remains of one of the harp strings. She tested an arrow against the makeshift bow. "Better than nothing," she said.

"We can't kill the Beast," Tom reminded her. "It's not his fault Malvel bewitched him."

Elenna lined up an arrow, and sent it into the tree beside Ursus. The Beast rocked backwards in panic, with Silver still leaping up at his scything claws. Storm closed in on the other side, wheeling his hooves to shepherd the Beast backwards. Tom's heart filled with pride to see the animals' courage. Ursus was off balance, and for the first time looked afraid. His eyes widened and his head jerked to take in the blur of the stallion's legs. Elenna shot another arrow, and this time caught the Beast's ankle. Ursus bellowed and dropped to all fours, pacing backwards to the edge of the water pool. Still though, his teeth were bared and his jaws foamed with thirst for blood.

Tom got to his feet and advanced, swinging his sword in dizzying arcs to confuse the Beast, but with his shield ready in case Ursus used his claws.

"Another arrow!" Tom shouted to Elenna.

With a roar, the Beast rose up, his claws rigid. At the same time, his back paw slipped on the muddy bank of the pool. Tom saw him topple backwards and an arrow whizzed past, thudding deep into the fur above his heart.

"No!" Elenna screamed as Ursus

crashed into the water, throwing up a
wave of spray. "I was aiming for his leg!"

Ursus floated in the water,
completely still, with blood trailing
from the arrow. Tom sank to his
knees on the bank, looking on
helplessly.

"What have we done?"

CHAPTER NINE

URSUS THE PROTECTOR

"I killed him," Elenna whispered. She dropped the bamboo bow to the ground.

Tom went to her side. "It's all right," he said. "He didn't give us any other choice." But he didn't feel at all sure he was right. In all the Beast Quests he'd completed, no Good Beast had ever died.

He heard a gentle splashing, and Elenna stiffened. "Tom!"

She pushed him away, and he followed her gaze back to the pool.

Ursus was stirring. The giant bear moved his head from side to side, and the orange spikes over his body seemed to shrink before Tom's eyes. In fact, the Beast's whole body seemed to be getting smaller, and his fur thickened to a rich brown pelt. When he was back to normal size, Ursus scrambled out of the pool, and shook the water off his fur. There wasn't even a sign of the arrow wound, and the bear yawned lazily.

"The curse has lifted," said Elenna. "He's a gentle giant again!"

"The harp's strings helped us push Ursus back until he couldn't fight any more," Tom said, thinking out loud.

"The harp was the best thing to defeat the evil coursing in Ursus's veins." Tom approached the bear with his hand out. Ursus lifted his nose and sniffed, then licked Tom's fingers. Even Silver and Storm approached the bear without fear.

Ursus turned and set off plodding along the path towards the caves. Tom and Elenna followed with the animals, past the destruction in the forest. As they came to the caves again, they heard a scream and rushed ahead. Myra was cowering in the mouth of one of the caves, and Brendan and Luke were holding branches sharpened into spears. Tom stood between them and the Beast.

"Ursus is good again!" he called out. "Malvel's enchantment is no more."

"You're sure?" called Brendan.

Before Tom could say anything more, Ursus sniffed the air, as though checking for attackers. Then he dipped his head, as though satisfied that no hostile strangers were near. Myra ran out, and buried her face in the fur on his belly.

Slowly Brendan and Luke came from the cave mouth, and gradually more faces appeared.

"They've cured Ursus!" shouted Luke.

Two other cave-dwellers brought out a huge pot of honey and laid it at Ursus's head. The bear rolled onto his stomach again, and began to lap at the golden liquid.

Luke slapped Tom and Elenna on the shoulders. "We owe you thanks," he said. "You've returned our protector to us. Join us for a feast. Stay a while. We can string you a hammock for the night."

Tom smiled. "This is only the start. If Malvel gets to the Eternal Flame, one Beast will be the least of our problems."

Brendan joined them. "Why do

you want to help Seraph so much?"
he asked.

Tom paused. He'd fought so many
Quests, saved many kingdoms. *I'm
not going to stop now*, he thought.
Seraph didn't deserve to suffer. And
Aduro… He'd bring his friend back
to life, no matter what it took.

"If I let Malvel conquer Seraph,
he'll destroy everything," he said at
last. "And there's a friend back home
who needs me to stop this evil
wizard." He looked towards the
dusky horizon, in the direction of the
mountain where the Eternal Flame
of Seraph awaited. "I should have
finished Malvel long ago."

"This time we won't let him get
away," said Elenna, her hand resting
in Silver's fur.

"We're only at the start of this

journey," Tom warned her.

Elenna shrugged. "It'll be the end, too," she said. "The end of Malvel."

Tom gazed out over the kingdom that had made them so welcome. He only hoped Elenna was right – if she was wrong, he wasn't sure he could keep anywhere safe any more.

He shook himself and forced a smile. "There'll be another Beast out there soon. Malvel's sure to create more."

"Then what are we waiting for?" Elenna asked, climbing into Storm's saddle. The forest people crowded round. Tom climbed into the saddle behind her.

"Goodbye!" he cried, as Storm set off, Silver racing beside them.

"Good luck!" the forest people called, as Ursus let out a gentle roar.

Tom waved goodbye. They were on their own again. And out there, somewhere, Malvel waited.

Join Tom on the next stage
of the Beast Quest when he meets

MINOS
THE DEMON BULL

Win an exclusive
Beast Quest T-shirt and goody bag!

In every Beast Quest book the Beast Quest logo is hidden in
one of the pictures. Find the logos in books 49 to 54
and make a note of which pages they appear on. Write the
six page numbers on a postcard and send it in to us.
Each month we will draw one winner to receive
a Beast Quest T-shirt and goody bag.

THE BEAST QUEST COMPETITION:
THE WARLOCK'S STAFF
Orchard Books
338 Euston Road, London NW1 3BH
Australian readers should email:
childrens.books@hachette.com.au

New Zealand readers should write to:
Beast Quest Competition
4 Whetu Place, Mairangi Bay, Auckland, NZ
or email: childrensbooks@hachette.co.nz

Only one entry per child.
Final draw: 4 September 2012

You can also enter this competition
via the Beast Quest website: www.beastquest.co.uk

All books priced at £4.99,
special bumper editions
priced at £5.99.

Orchard Books are available from all good bookshops, or can
be ordered from our website: www.orchardbooks.co.uk,
or telephone 01235 827702, or fax 01235 8227703.

Series 9: THE WARLOCK'S STAFF
COLLECT THEM ALL!

Malvel is up to his evil tricks again! The fate of all the lands is in Tom's hands...

URSUS
THE CLAWED ROAR
978 1 40831 316 9

MINOS
THE DEMON BULL
978 1 40831 317 6

KORAKA
THE WINGED ASSASSIN
978 1 40831 318 3

SILVER
THE WILD TERROR
978 1 40831 319 0

SPIKEFIN
THE WATER KING
978 1 40831 320 6

TORPIX
THE TWISTING SERPENT
978 1 40831 321 3